FAMILY TIES
Raising Wild Babies

written and illustrated by

Jennifer Owings Dewey

Marshall Cavendish
New York

In memory of Sally Carrighar,
an early inspiration,

and for C.K.B., a friend for life

Text and illustrations copyright © 1998 by Jennifer Owings Dewey
All rights reserved.
Marshall Cavendish, 99 White Plains Road, Tarrytown, New York 10591

Library of Congress Cataloging-in-Publication Data
Dewey, Jennifer. Family ties: raising wild babies / Jennifer Dewey.
p. cm
Includes Index.
Summary: A collection of stories about a great horned owl, a mother coyote,
a bobcat, a one-eyed raven, and a bear cub.
ISBN 0-7614-5037-8
1. Animals—Juvenile fiction. 2. Children's stories, American.
[1. Animals—Fiction. 2. Short stories.] I. Title.
PZ10.3.D52An 1999 [Fic]—dc21 98-5201 CIP AC

The text of this book is set in 12 point Berkeley Old Style Medium.
The illustrations are rendered in pencil.
Book design by Carol Matsuyama
Printed in the United States of America
1 3 5 6 4 2

Contents

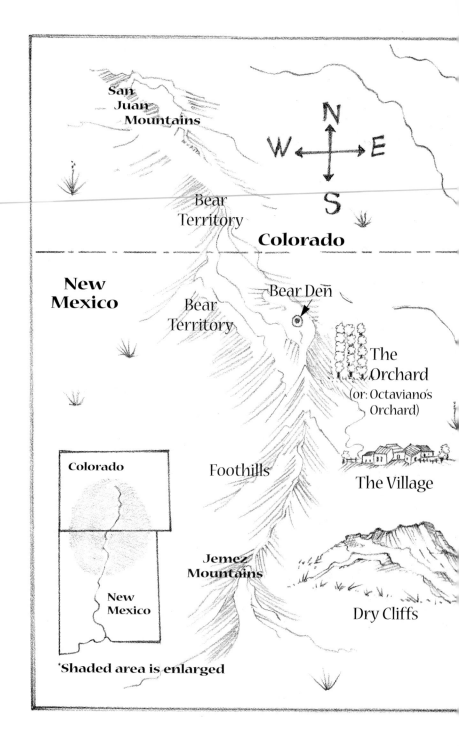

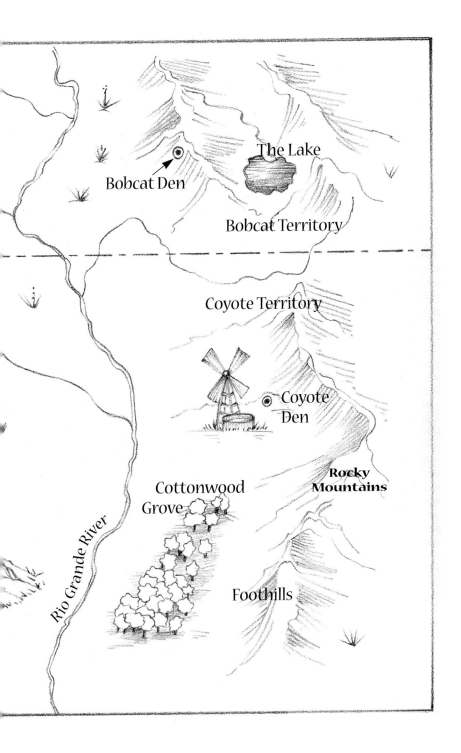

Introduction

The first time I saw the great horned owl flying through the cottonwood grove I figured the bird was a visitor passing through and not likely to stay. But I decided I would go back to see if I could spot the owl again, and I did. I went back day after day and watched, hiding from the owl at first. I soon realized the owl had a nest in the grove, and young. She was thin and bedraggled. From her appearance, I wondered if she might be starving.

Observing the mother owl, seeing her loyally come and go to and from her nest, made me believe she was doing her best, thinking hard, trying to save her owlets. The sacrifices she made for her young seemed to reflect the way human mothers act if their babies are threatened.

Wild animal behavior can be so like human behavior that we wonder how much an animal thinks or doesn't think. It is one of the great mysteries that arises when observing wild animal families: how smart are they? Do animals have intelligence? When we observe family ties and friendship bonds that resemble our own it is tempting to make assumptions about animal emotions.

While they can learn and adapt in remarkable ways, wild animals act primarily out of instinct, powerful drives bred into them over time. They lack the ability to think broadly and deeply. Wild creatures have traits inherited from their ancestors, and their responses are "hard wired" into their brains. If these have worked to keep a species going, they are saved and repeated in each new generation.

Human beings think about the world around them, pondering the meaning of life, inventing rockets and sending them to the moon, using powerful imaginations to write books and paint pictures. Other animals respond to their world in simpler, more direct ways. Their behavior is based mostly on the urge to survive and protect young.

Each of the following stories is based on my observations while spending time in the area near my home. When I followed the female coyote and her pups across an open plain, I worked hard to imagine myself in her skin. I let myself be seen, hoping she would adjust to my presence. It always surprises me how far my imagination can carry me into a coyote's world. This is one of the joys of going out to spend days, even weeks, in the wilderness.

I have done the same pretending with the ravens, owls, bobcats, and bears. When I try to sense what is "on their minds," I feel closer to each, even with the separation their wildness creates.

The gap between human and wild animals seems to shrink when we watch families work together to raise their young. They become part of the larger family of life on Earth. We see them dream and play, and we come as close as we ever will to understanding their wildness.

Even with the differences between "us" and them," observing wild families shows us how alike we are, sometimes in surprising ways. I wrote these stories in the spirit of curiosity about the kinships we share.

All of the stories are true and actually happened in the environments described.

A Mother Owl's Story

The great horned owl stood motionless, her yellow eyes unblinking. She gripped the branch of the cottonwood tree with her talons and listened for sounds in the night, the rustling of rodents hunting on the ground.

A disk of stiff, densely packed feathers covered the owl's face. The shape and size of these helped funnel noises from the outside world to the owl's ears, two holes hidden beneath layers of feathers on the sides of her skull. The owl's sense of hearing was acute enough for her to hear the shrew scampering under dry leaves seventy yards from her nest tree.

The owl leaned forward and dropped off the branch, falling for more than a foot before rushing air under her wings supported her weight. Her wings sliced the air without a sound. The owl's large eyes absorbed what little light there was in the cottonwood grove, but she relied on her hearing more than her eyes to find where the shrew was running.

She swept through the cottonwoods, a feather-draped ghost in controlled flight. Seconds before landing she thrust her wings behind her head. She came down with her spine in a half-moon bend, talons spread.

The owl's kill was so quick, the skinny-tailed shrew surely felt nothing when it died. With the prey clutched in her talons the mother owl rested on the ground. She gulped air into her lungs in shallow gasps.

The owl was slowly starving to death. Spring rains had failed to come to the cottonwood grove, a hundred-acre forest of trees in the foothills of the New Mexico mountains. The country for miles around was parched and dusty for lack of moisture. Many animals had left the grove to search for food elsewhere.

The owl stayed. Her bulky stick nest, once a raven's nest, was home to three hungry owlets. The male great horned owl, the female's mate, had left, not able to capture enough food for himself and the owlets. His instinct to survive, even at the price of abandoning his family, pulled him away.

The stillness of the night deepened after the owl killed the shrew. Hairy wolf spiders and shiny black beetles hid under dead leaves with their bodies rigid, alert to danger.

When the owl was ready to lift into the air she pushed at the earth with her feet and reached up with her broad wings, the lifeless shrew dangling from her beak.

At the sight of their mother the owlets burst into sharp, shrill cries of hunger, tiny explosions of sound that disturbed the quiet of the grove. They lunged in her direction, desperate to snap at the prey she carried. In their eagerness they nearly tumbled out of the nest. Before she fed them, the mother owl bit the shrew into small pieces. She gave a meager portion to each owlet.

After eating, the owlets lapsed into a restless slumber, their pin-feathered bodies heaped together in a space the size of a large soup bowl. The nest was littered with discarded feathers and a scattering of the bones of prey animals. The mother owl stepped out of the nest and fell away into the night, her search for food a constant task.

In the gloom of the final hour before dawn the mother owl's flight took her to the edge of the grove. She spotted a diamondback rattlesnake slithering across the ground and fell on it in a flash. Great horned owls are among the few creatures on earth capable of taking on a prey animal as dangerous as a rattlesnake.

She loomed out of the shadows, a whirl of dusky feathers with sharp talons ready to grasp the snake's scaly body. When the owl landed she tightened her toe muscles and secured her grip, forcing the points of her talons deep into the snake's flesh. The snake turned its muscular length and thrust its face into the owl's feathered chest. The owl felt the snake's fangs burn into her, twin needles delivering fire.

The owl's attack and the snake's strike took less than thirty seconds.

Badly wounded and in a fury of rage, the owl caught the snake's weaving neck in her beak and twisted her head abruptly. The snake's spine snapped like a twig. The battle was over. The owl had won. The rattlesnake lay looped on the ground in a death coil, a section of its body circling the owl's legs.

With a thrumming heartbeat, her brain awash with pain, the owl's concentration slipped. She closed her eyes and dropped her head to her chest, losing consciousness just as the sun rose.

She lay slack on the ground when the first light of a new day swept across the tops of the cottonwoods. The owl rallied after long moments passed. She regained enough strength to press her legs and feet to the earth and bring herself into the air. The snake hung loosely from her ankles.

The owl flew with pain-dimmed eyes and slammed into the side of the nest as the last of her strength gave out. The owlets greeted her with the usual shrieks and cries of hunger. She ignored them.

Her three-pound weight landed on top of their quivering bodies in a disorganized heap of feathers. She was soon asleep, lost in a venom-induced coma, one that would last five days.

The snake hung like a section of discarded garden hose across the top of the nest. The owlets ripped and tore at the snake's flesh, filling their bellies with its meat while their mother slept.

On the morning of the sixth day the mother owl woke up. The rising sun cast pale yellow streamers of light through the leaves of the cottonwoods. She opened her eyes and closed them immediately. The intensity of the sun's rays made her eyes ache. Her head throbbed with pain.

A fire raged in her. She moved her wings and twisted her head and shoulders. Her lower body did not respond to her brain commands. The owl might have recovered fully from a light infusion of rattlesnake venom, but too great an amount had entered her body. The snake's venom had paralyzed her from the chest down.

The mother owl nudged her babies with her beak. They slept peacefully, bellies full and rounded by their snake-meat meals. She nipped and tore at the remains of the snake, swallowing a few rancid bites. She was thirsty. She'd gone without food for almost six days.

The mother owl flexed her shoulders and lifted her wings to test the use of her muscles. Her movements dislodged what remained of the snake, skin and bones in the mid-section with chunks of rotting meat at both ends. It fell and landed on the dusty ground with a hollow thud.

A young raccoon, its ribs outlined sharply under a speckled gray coat, took the snake's rotting carcass in its teeth. While chewing the snake, the raccoon picked up the aroma of owl. The raccoon scrambled up the trunk of the cottonwood. When it came to the nest it met the mother owl's glaring eyes.

The two animals faced each other over the top of the nest. The owl leaned forward, bringing herself half out of the nest bowl. She expressed her rage by hissing and clicking. Both animals lost their balance and fell as a pair of stones would, tumbling head over tail and hitting the ground hard. The instant they landed the raccoon jumped up and ran.

The owl discovered she could not fly. She was stranded at the base of the tree, unable to return to the nest. She tossed side to side for all the hot hours of the day, thrashing and twisting, trying desperately to force her body to obey her will.

In the night she listened to the pitiful whines and cries of her owlets when they woke up wondering where their mother was. The sounds were a trigger that renewed her determination to lift her body and fly.

A pair of coyotes passing through the grove smelled easy prey. The two padded close to the tree, silent as smoke. The owl roused herself to a frenzy of clicking and clattering, driving the predators away.

She survived the first night and two more. On the third night the male, her mate, appeared out of long shadows cast by the setting sun. The carcass of a freshly killed skunk hung from his talons.

The male owl had eaten well during his absence. His feathers shone. His body was sleek and round. There was a glow in his yellow eyes the female recognized. She buzzed low in her throat, a signal that told him she welcomed him back.

The female snatched hungrily at the scraps of skunk the male offered, the cramp of hunger like a twisted wire in her gut. The male flew up to the nest and fed the owlets. Their dull eyes brightened once they were revived by the food in their bellies.

The owl pair had been together five years. Their bond was strong. The male stayed on, leaving his mate only to hunt for food. He flew long distances to find enough prey to feed his family. He was often gone for more than a day. He always reappeared. He had the strength for these journeys, something his mate no longer possessed.

Two days after the male's return an early summer storm brought a downpour in the night. Thunder filled the canyons with echoing roars that boomed down the mountain slopes. Lightning flickered yellow and electric blue in the eastern sky. The rain swept through the trees in shimmering gray waves, sounding a steady pattern of beats as it fell.

The storm brought relief to every living thing. Rainwater spilled down the mother owl's throat. The life-giving moisture offered some small measure of strength.

The next morning the grove stirred with the sounds of animals roused by hunger and want. The owl saw the shadows of a pair of coyotes slipping through the trees, their sensitive noses leading them to underground mouse burrows.

When darkness came a bobcat crept through the grove on well-furred feet. The owl drove the bobcat away with a frenzy of hissing, clicking, and buzzing. Raccoons hunted both day and night for insects, lizards, and frogs, and plucked ripening berries off juniper trees.

The owlets gained strength quickly, with meals brought by their father three, four, or five times each day. They began to catch up with themselves, gaining weight with every bite of food dropped into their throats.

On a sunny afternoon after a night of rain they were ready to stand on a branch in the nest tree, wobbly with excitement, and take their first practice flight.

The first two made safe passage through the air, dropping in long glides from the nest tree to the ground below. They were still scrawny for their age, but their wiry bodies and growing wings served them well.

The third owlet was the smallest, the runt. This one dropped from the cottonwood branch and lost control. It landed in a whimpering heap with its beak pressed into soil still damp with rain.

The father owl stood on a branch in a tree some distance away from the nest and lured the smallest owlet to another try. The lure was a freshly killed gopher he dangled from his beak. The trick worked.

The little owl soared through the air in a slow-motion glide, avoiding collision with tree trunks, its fear apparent only in its wide, staring eyes. It landed on two feet, legs bent, no worse for the experience. The male dropped to the ground to reward the young owlet with a hefty portion of the gopher.

The female died on a moonless night with the male, her mate, next to her. His food offerings and watchful guarding were not enough to save her. The snake's venom had destroyed nerves and blood vessels in her lower body. Her heart gave out because it failed to receive a healthy, steady flow of blood.

The three young owls kept silent company with their father on nights of hunting. Their skills at capturing prey were honed by watching the older male, and imitating what he did. It was some time before any of the three took hunting trips alone. They killed small prey at first, mice, insects, and voles, leaving the larger animals to their more experienced elder.

It was winter when the three young owls flew away forever, to live apart from their father in new territory.

The male might find another mate. Only time would tell. He would remain in the grove for, whatever happened, the hundred-acre cottonwood forest was his home.

The Coyote Family

The coyote knew the sensation in her middle, the cramps and shooting pains that began high in her chest and traveled down to her tail. She had given birth to four litters in ten years.

The contractions came in waves. The regularity of them brought tears to her eyes. She was getting old. Her ability to endure the pains of birth was less than it had been.

When the first pup slipped out, the coyote knew a brief spell of relief. Her knees buckled and she collapsed on the den floor. She flopped over on her right side and stayed still, breathing in rapid gasps. The second pup came, and this time the pains subsided even more.

The coyote lay flat out, her rib cage outlined under the stretched skin of her tawny hide. She breathed evenly, allowing the noise of it to fill the den chamber. She slid her moist tongue over the surfaces of her teeth. The third pup was born.

She winced and closed her eyes. The last spasms of pain fell away from her consciousness as a leaf in a breeze flutters to the ground. Her ordeal was over.

There were three little ones. In the past she had given birth to as many as six. She hunched up and twisted her lower body around to reach the newborns. She began to clean them.

The old female extended her pink tongue to lick the noses, eyes, and mouths of her pups, making sure they breathed with clean, smooth gulps of air. She fluffed the hairs on their backs and sides until their pale coats were fluffy and dry. She snapped the umbilical cords with her teeth and chewed and swallowed the afterbirth. Any nourishment she could find she took eagerly, and the afterbirth was a source of protein.

When she finished cleaning and drying her babies the mother coyote stood on all fours and scratched at the hard, packed floor of the den with her toenails. She scrubbed at the blood and fluids of the birth that stained the dirt. She did this to help hide the raw, rank smell, to lessen the chances a bold bobcat or mountain lion might wander by and be drawn by its nose to enter the den.

When their mother lay down once more the pups nibbled and poked at her belly, toothless mouths searching for teats. They crawled blindly, the instinct to suckle born in them.

The mother coyote mouthed and tugged at them

gently with her teeth. She pushed each one with her nose to direct its progress. Her milk was coming in. Instinct told her she would have a good supply for her young.

Before long each pup held a smooth, rubbery nipple clasped in its jaws. The steady rhythm of nursing noises filled the den chamber. The little ones sucked, filling their empty bellies with rich, warm milk. The old female cleaned herself, aware of sore muscles and a burning under her tail. The pups had made safe passage into the world. The sounds of their feeding lulled her. She closed her eyes and covered her nose with her paws. She sighed deeply and fell asleep.

A male coyote, the female's mate, paced at the den entrance. He held his head down, his nose almost touching the ground. He grumbled and whined with nervous impatience.

The male was seven, three years younger than the old female. He had fallen into a restless state once the arrival of the pups was near. Litters coming made him edgy. He had been the female's mate through two earlier litters. He relied on her for direction as she was the dominant one of the pair. Without the attention he was used to from her the male lapsed into an irritable moodiness.

The male poked his nose into the den entrance, risking the female's anger in his eagerness for a signal from her. He whimpered in a high, singsong voice.

The female heard him and she roused herself, coming up on all fours slowly because of the aching pains in her back. The pups slipped from her teats when she stood. She nuzzled and licked them. They squeaked in protest, but were soon curled in a furry heap of bodies, sound asleep.

At the opening to the den, the female growled at her mate. She pushed at him with her head, butting him in the ribs. Her sounds were a language the male understood. She told him all was well. He could quit whimpering. He should go away and stop bothering her, go hunting and find something for his family to eat.

A few weeks before the pups were born the female had driven the male out of the den. She would not welcome him back until the pups had opened their eyes and were scrambling out of the entrance to greet the world. Only then could he reenter the den and sleep with his family.

The male's task was to feed and protect his mate, to hunt and bring food to her. For several weeks he had deposited small prey at the den entrance, rabbits and little piles of meadow mice, which his mate snapped up and ate.

Now the male loped off, reassured by the female's growl. She lost sight of him quickly because the color of his coat perfectly matched the sea of sagebrush-covered plain.

The coyote pair claimed a territory that spread as far as they could travel easily in a day. They knew every hill, ridge, and sinkhole, the best hunting, and the best places to hide or take shelter from storms. They walked the same pathways so often their feet had worn deep ruts in the soil. At times the two met other coyotes, small family groups crossing east to west, or south to north. They shared their territory now and again. Mostly it belonged to them alone.

Their source of water was a few yards from the den, an abandoned windmill with a water-filled stock tank at the base. The tank and the windmill were relics from the past, left to rust on overgrazed rangeland. The ancient pumping system was primitive, but it still worked.

The coyotes could watch the flaring metal blades at the top of the windmill tower spin lazily most days, and hear a dull clank-clank-clank noise that turned to a screaming whine on days the wind was up. Pipes carried fresh, clean water from deep in the ground up into the tank.

The metal sides of the tank were pockmarked with bullet holes. Water spilled from the holes to form puddles on the ground around the tank. Many animals visited the place to drink, bathe, and refresh themselves, or to prey on others who came.

When the male disappeared the female moved a little distance from the den to relieve herself. She went to the tank to drink, her belly rumbling with emptiness.

She pulled her lips back and bared her teeth to pluck at tender grasses growing around the edge of the tank. The soft green stems tasted sweet and fresh. She felt better after nibbling, and after taking long gulps of cold water into her throat and stomach.

The male walked soundlessly, leaving paw prints on the crumbly soil. He paused to mark his territory, urinating on clumps of sagebrush or scratching at the earth with his sharp toenails.

He hunted until moonrise, capturing seven gray field mice with pink noses and white feet, and one gopher. He forced the food to the back of his mouth with his tongue and bit down hard with his molars before swallowing.

His hunger satisfied, he lay down on a patch of dry grass and rubbed his belly against the scratchiness of it. Small rodents scurried close. He could hear their squeaks and the faint pattering of running feet. He snapped at three and killed them instantly.

He didn't eat his catch. He stood up, shook the dust out of his coat, and picked up the dead mice in his front teeth. He set off toward the den with the rodents dangling from his jaws.

The old female sat grooming at the den entrance. She licked the long cream-colored hairs under her tail, chewing at matted and dried blood. The look in her eyes was calm but intense, hunger a tight band across her middle.

The male cut a sharp right around a sage and approached. He dropped the mice at her feet. The female snapped at the food, her greenish-yellow eyes aglow. The pair rubbed noses before the male went to his sleeping place, a den nearby. The female returned to her pups.

There were two females and one male in the litter. The pups grew quickly. They were healthy and strong and well cared for by their experienced mother.

At five weeks their coats were the color of butterscotch, thick with hairs as soft as goose down. Their vision was blurred, but their eyes were wide open. They played roughly, nipping, biting, and snapping at each other in the darkness of the den.

One day when they were six weeks old, their tiny, sensitive noses led them up the tunnel to the surface, to greet the sun and breathe fresh air for the first time. The male was not as large for his age as his sisters. These two rolled in the dust like a pair of rubber balls wearing fur coats. The male did not lack strengh, he was just built small. He moved with grace and quickness, showing the skills of a natural hunter early on.

The male pup followed his mother everywhere, nipping at her tail, curling himself at her ankles, and biting her toes. He was persistent about nursing, tugging at his mother's teats long after his sisters were weaned. The old female indulged him. She growled at the females, snapping if they tried to nurse, allowing the little male to have his way.

When the pups were twelve weeks old they joined their parents on a hunt. They were aware enough to follow commands instantly, to walk in silence through the sage, and make themselves scarce if need be.

At dusk a night of hunting began. The pair of adults climbed to a low rise where juniper and sage offered cover. They took turns lifting their noses to the sky to yip and sing calls that carried across the plains like a shrill, high wind. Coyotes on distant ridges heard the songs and answered with yips and barks of their own.

On their first venture into the darkness, the young male kept close to his mother, brushing her flanks and nibbling on her ears when she rested. The daughters trailed their father. When the serious hunting began and the adults stalked a rabbit or pounced on a young skunk, snapping a neck or a spine to make a kill, the little ones stood aside, quietly watching and learning.

It was during a night of hunting that one of the females was lost. She lagged behind the others in the darkness and when the buzzing of the rattlesnake came, it was too late for the old female or the male to do anything to save her from the strike.

Winter arrived on the prairie. Gusts of frigid wind blew out of the southwest. Snow fell lightly at first, a scattering of white flakes that melted the moment the sun was out. Then the big storms came, those that lasted days instead of hours. Snow drifted before the wind in swirling clouds that hung in the air, blotting out the world before settling on the ground to conceal every beetle trail, every rodent track and mouse burrow.

It was after a three-day storm that the song dog family emerged from the den, their eyes showing hunger, their bellies hollow and sore, their tempers short. All shared an instinctive yearning to shake their coats, winter-dense with extra layers of fine hairs, and feel the sun's pale warmth on their noses.

It was the first winter for the young ones. The snow

was thrilling to them. Both young animals burst from the den with explosive eagerness, racing up and down hillsides and looping around bushes. The cold, deep whiteness of the drifts was fun to plow into. The ridges were raceways where limbs, stiff and cramped from forced seclusion in the den, found welcome release. The young animals lay on their backs on beds of white flakes and pumped the air with their legs, yowling with the satisfaction of high-energy play.

Both parents watched from a little distance, until the father joined in the fun, unable to resist the joy of it. He started a game of chase that wore the youngsters out.

When he was tired he slumped down on his stomach. The pups copied his position, staring expectantly to see what he would do next, breathing hard, their amber eyes glittering brightly.

When their play was done the family scattered in four directions, hunting for what they could find: a few scrawny rodents tunneling under the snow or dried berries plucked from junipers.

The sun slipped past midday and the coyotes rejoined. As a pack they loped westward, going single file with the old female in the lead.

In the hour before dusk the four lay down to rest under a chamisa bush, its branches droopy from the weight of new snow. Before long the young male, restless to explore, went a short distance away to dig in the snow, probing its depths with his nose and paws. Suddenly, and with no warning, he screamed. The awful sound came from high in his chest, in a space near his heart.

The old female ran to him snarling with her teeth bared, as she would do when driving off an attacking mountain lion or bear. There was no enemy, nothing she could see or smell to have brought on the scream he had made.

She grabbed the loose neck-skin behind his head in her jaws and pulled him across the ground, as if trying to separate his small body from what was hurting him. The intensity of his howling increased.

She stopped her tugging and stood quietly watching him. His howls became weaker. She nibbled at one of his ears, and he whimpered.

The father started to approach, his head low. He backed off quickly when the old female growled at him viciously. The female pup sat on the snowy ground twenty yards away, her shoulders slumped, her head low.

The old female tried something new. She dug at the snow that covered the young male, moving with slow deliberate care, working to expose the pup's limbs. In this way she discovered the cause of his agony.

He had become tangled in a ring of barbed wire hidden under the snow, rusty with years of lying on the ground, but still dangerous for its spiral of pointed barbs, sharp even after years of neglect.

With round, fearful eyes the pup watched his mother lick his body clean of the white froth that concealed his wounds. The old female knew the few gashes dripping red blood on the snow were not just cause for the screams she had heard. When she poked her nose under the pup's belly to urge him to his feet it became clear his right back leg was broken. The wire hung on the leg at the break site, where the bone now bent strangely backward.

The old female bit and chewed at the wire to free the pup's leg, ignoring the pitiful cries he made, bloodying her mouth in the process. When the pup was free of the wire, she gently rolled him over so his broken leg faced the sky. She pushed snow on the break with her nose, to slow the flow of blood and ease the pain, and then lay across him, draping the middle of his body with her warmth. She placed one of her front legs under his head to elevate it.

The others watched, the father yipping nervous cries of alarm. These were short, brief bursts of sound that came from low in his chest. The young female cried gently and steadily, like a baby caught in the rain not knowing which way to turn.

The sun set, the wind came up, and the old female signaled with her voice, telling her mate and the female pup to join her where she lay, to press their bodies close and make heat. They did as she directed.

The old female stayed with the pup for three days. She never once left him, unless to take steps away to urinate, or dig at roots below the hard, frozen ground, which she chewed and swallowed for the sake of the little nourishment they offered. She lapped snow into the pup's mouth, and did the same for herself, to quench the thirst they both suffered.

After the first night, when morning came, it was certain the female would stay with the injured pup. Her mate reluctantly led the female pup back to the den and safety. He did this because the old female ordered him to. In sending her mate back to the den the old female gave him a strong signal: do not return, even with offerings of food Instinct told the old female this. She knew it must be herself who remained alone and exposed to guard the pup.

The father was again restless, as he had been the day the pups were born. He was expert at playing games, roaming free, and taking orders from the female. He must now spend his energy and time looking after the female pup.

Vultures soared above, circling endlessly, drawn by the smell of blood. Magpies, long tails flashing in the sun, landed and bounced on the snowy ground, anticipating the taste of fresh meat. Ravens came in dark flocks, eyes eager and bright, their constant calls a symphony of rude noises. The old coyote quickly grew tired of their cackling. She growled and snarled to drive them off.

On the fourth day the old female nudged the pup, coaxing him with soft, throaty murmurs, urging him to stand. He winced, cried, and did as she willed. He discovered that three of his legs worked well enough, though they were stiff and sore from cold. The broken leg was bent into a hooked position. This leg was dead but the rest of him lived.

In a month's time the pup had mastered a bobbing gait that took him anywhere he needed to go. His limp did not hinder him. His ordeal deepened his connection to his mother. He was her companion now, in all but the matter of mating. They spent their idle hours together and hunted as a pair. When the old female's mate came close, whining and wanting to nuzzle her behind the ears or groom her coat by tugging at burrs and ticks, she refused him.

Winter eased into spring. When the male tried to mate with the old female she snarled meanly, snapped her jaws, and bared her teeth. Her furious rejection sent him running into the sage with his tail between his legs.

He returned to try again, aware she was prone to bad tempers. Each time she drove him off. She would have nothing to do with him. Finally this was clear, even to him. Her time for breeding was past. The male could not fathom this, but the old female knew. She knew by the ache in her joints, the stiffness in her spine, and the mist in her eyes.

In late spring the male went on a hunting trip from which he never returned. His family heard his yipping songs in the night, but they never set eyes on him again.

In the year that followed, the daughter, with her mother and brother, went on two- and three-day hunting trips that often took them one hundred miles between dusk and sunrise.

Then came the time the old female and her lame son were together alone, just the two of them; there were no others. The daughter had found a mate and was gone to another place, a territory far away that was traveled by the coyote pack she joined.

The old female aged steadily. Her crankiness worsened as her joints became swollen and sore. Her eyes wore the creamy white film of blindness. She slept most days—and did little else.

The young male hunted for the pair of them. Long ago his mother had chewed and swallowed his food, then regurgitated it out of her stomach into his hungry mouth. Now he did this for her. When she could not drag herself to the water tank, he sucked water into his mouth and came to where she lay and spilled water down her throat. He was her guardian and protector, as she had been for him.

For three days the smell of her death was strong, and he stayed at her side, not leaving to eat, drink, or even relieve himself. He watched and waited, keeping a vigil until her breathing stopped. He dragged her into the den chamber, down the dim tunnel to the room where he and his sisters had been born. This dark, safe place was her tomb.

He left the den by the water tank a few days later, weaving invisibly through the sage on familiar paths. The sage was blooming. The sweet heady smell of the tiny pink flowers made him dizzy. He moved in his own odd way, bobbing like a large, furry quail, his useless back leg bent under his belly. He turned his face away from the den by the water tank, to discover a new life in another place.

Bobcat Mountain

An autumn storm had dropped new snow in a range of mountains where three peaks rise to fourteen thousand feet. When the clouds moved west the snow pack shimmered in the sun.

A thousand feet below the snow-covered peaks, a young male bobcat moved along the lower edge of a scree slope edged by a thick pine forest. He stepped carefully to avoid cutting tender toe pads on the sharp stones that make up the rockfall. He sniffed the air repeatedly, his nose high, his whiskers twitching. The bobcat tried to locate the familiar scent trail of his mother and twin sister.

The bobcat stopped and looked down at the bottom of the rockfall. A stream of water trickled out from under the gray expanse of stones, water draining down the mountain from the snow pack above.

The bobcat twisted his body in a sharp turn. His furred gray-black hide slipped and slid over his bones like a piece of fabric. His shoulder blades rose and fell with every step. His rounded ears, topped with tufts of hair, stuck straight up. The bobcat put his nose to the ground when he detected a faint scent he knew by heart.

He followed the smell and stopped where the water spilled from the rockfall. The small stream continued beyond the rocks, traveling a slender course through a grassy meadow where it flowed into a lake. The bobcat lost the trail but soon picked it up again. Once more the aromas of his relatives were heavy in his nostrils. His heart beat faster. He was filled with anticipation.

The bobcat rememberd a sunning place his family favored, on the north side of the lake. He kept his nose to the scent, which led him toward the spot.He was following old smells from days past, not new ones that would reveal where his mother and sister were.

The young bobcat did not seek his father. The adult male had left the rest of the family weeks before, to live the solitary, roaming life common to adult male bobcats.

At the sunning spot he dropped on his belly. The grass was flattened, pressed down from bobcat bodies constantly sleeping on it. The bobcat scratched at the grass with his front claws and took up bits of shed fur. He snapped at these with his teeth and licked his face with his tongue. He half-closed his eyes. Fragments of memory, the events of the day before, came together and took shape in his brain.

He was with his mother and sister at the lake. After an hour of wrestling and playing he settled for a nap, his sister on one side, his mother on the other.

The three of them woke up to a crackling, booming roar that sounded like summer thunder. It wasn't thunder. The earth beneath their feet quivered and trembled. In seconds the roar grew louder, more intense. The mother launched her body into a run. The twins did their best to keep up with her.

An avalanche of stones had been set in motion high above a lake, a fall of rock loosened when a boulder slipped off its base. The tumble of shale shattered the peace of the afternoon and sent countless animals fleeing for their lives.

The three bobcats dashed as fast as their legs could carry them, barely keeping ahead of the approaching earthquake of rock cascading down the mountain. Showers of stones hit the ground around them, threatening to knock them senseless and break their bones.

As they ran they became separated. The young male, in confusion and terror, went a different direction from his mother and sister.

When the avalanche stopped and the forest was quiet again it was as if nothing had happened. The difference, now, was that the young bobcat was alone for the first time in his life. His mother and sister were nowhere in sight. He searched for them until until dark. He cried and whined in a pathetic voice. His yowls and meows revealed his presence to every animal nearby.

At dusk he circled back to the lake and creeped on his stomach into the shelter of a hollow rank-smelling log near the water. The area around the lake was home to him. Every landmark was potent with memories of the hours he had spent with his family in this place. He slept soundly in the log.

At first light he was awake. He crawled out of the log and shook himself. He licked his paws with his tongue and rubbed his face and ears. He cleaned himself along the line of his belly, from under his tail to below his chin, and the sweet odor of moisture off the lake filled his nose. He became aware of another smell, a sharp feline scent he had never caught in his nostrils before. He explored the edge of the lake and sniffed out tracks in the spongy mud, the prints of a grown bobcat. He did not recognize the tracks.

Perhaps the young bobcat would not know one track from another, unless it were his father's, his mother's, or the paw prints of his sister. He was still young and without experience in life, too young to fathom the mystery of unfamiliar tracks or know how to react when he saw them.

He was both curious and afraid, nervous but eager.

When the acrid scent of the stranger-cat seemed to fade, he concentrated on snapping at bees hovering over seed heads in the reeds by the water.

The young bobcat reacted to simple urges: hunger, thirst, the urge to play, and the tug of yearning he experienced, loneliness for the companionship of his mother and sister.

To satisfy hunger he caught meadow mice, five of them, and swallowed them almost without chewing. To quench his thirst he sipped icy water from the lake. When he was through chasing bumblebees he was ready to set off searching again for his family.

The sun was well above the peaks when he walked into the coolness of the pine forest, once more focused on finding the scent trail made by his mother and sister. He had barely crossed into the shade of the forest when he was startled by a sound. It was the rustle of an animal in motion. When the rustling stopped, an eerie silence fell. No bird twittered. No cricket chirped.

The bobcat inched forward, his curiosity stronger than his impulse to flee. He peered into the hazy gloom, a shadow world dimmed by pine and spruce branches blocking the sun's light.

His gaze slid over a seemingly blank curtain of forest and suddenly he saw a face. A bobcat was watching him.

He was afraid. In fear, his joints went cold and stiff. Nothing in his nearly one year of living told him what to do. He stood as if made of stone, staring at the face, the two yellow eyes, until the image dissolved into nothing and vanished.

The young bobcat sat on his haunches, his brain trying to gather in what he had seen, or not seen. Did he imagine it? After some moments he was up and moving, making his way to a place on the mountain where he had known good times with his family. Yearning for a particular reassurance, he headed for the den where he was born.

As nervous energy replaced terror, the impulse to play seized him. He climbed the mountain in leaps and bounds, his muscular body stretched like a wire, his speed surprising. His run was more than getting up the mountain. It was the pure joy of movement. He achieved the upper reaches of the incline in seconds, as few other creatures would be capable of doing.

The bobcat whipped his body into a bower of mountain mahogany, a thick stand growing against a big gray boulder. He dived nose first into a dark, moist hole under the bulge of rock. It was the den.

The den was empty. He was as much alone as before. He was aware, from the smell of the hollow under the boulder, that it had been empty a long time. Odors he knew well—comfortable smells—lingered in the den. He checked every inch of the floor with his nose, sniffing and snuffling. He licked and pawed at dead leaves and rotting pine needles, tasting with his rough pink tongue what he pulled up with his claws. His examination of the den included wriggling on his back, his four paws smacking at empty space. With every move he reclaimed the den chamber and made it his own once more.

He rolled over and settled motionless on his belly. His brain absorbed the reality of his new existence, his separation from his family. There was no mother for him to snuggle next to, no sister to tease and spar with. No father. The bobcat heard the whine of the wind. He cringed and closed his eyes. The roar was cruel in his ears.

Another sound came, the high, shrill crying of a bobcat. The young bobcat shuddered, his eyes wide and staring. His muscles tensed with fear. He was being trailed, followed, pursued. He was not alone after all. The enemy was there, outside the den, near and threatening.

He found enough courage to scrunch on his stomach to the den opening and look out. His ears laid flat against his head, his chin pressed the damp ground firmly. Pinned by fear to the ground, he saw nothing but the bases and stumps of pines and the litter of the forest floor.

He was afraid to venture farther out of the den, too much a baby missing the comfort of his mother. The wind howled with new energy, and he turned back into the dark safety of the den to curl himself into a ball. He had one sure hiding place, and that was enough for now.

When he stopped shivering he fell into a restless sleep. He had dreams of the enemy cat, the one with yellow eyes that shone too large in a fierce, ugly face. The cat's teeth were bared. The fangs were positioned to rip into him.

A winter storm passed across the mountains while the bobcat slept. Clouds wrapped the peaks. The storm started with heavy rains that pounded the earth. Bolts of

lightning struck, shattering granite into gray dust.

At nightfall the rain turned to snow, peaceful, soft, and soundless. The snow floated gently across the range, falling all night long. It formed deep layers on the boulder fields, filling the spaces between stones. In the silence of the snow's fall the air froze hard.

One animal remained in motion in spite of the weather. It was the sly, partly hidden bobcat of the forest, he with the watching yellow eyes—the same bobcat that had screamed into the roar of the wind just as the storm arrived.

The bobcat was grizzled and ancient in bobcat time. He weighed twenty-seven sinewy pounds and stood nineteen inches tall. He knew his way around the mountain blind.

He had survived by fighting off all intruders, including mountain lions and bears. He was an expert at eating tender lambs taken from flocks in the high meadows, lambs he had snagged with his claws in the darkness of a summer night while the shepherd and his dogs were helpless to hinder the slaughter. He had pulled coyote pups from dens and snatched baby badgers in broad daylight.

He was a wanderer, a loner. He hunched up against a rock outcrop or found a sheltered ledge for sleep, even in the worst weather. A mass of patchy scar tissue from a bullet wound showed pink and gray on his right shoulder, the result of a shot fired to drive him away from a pen full of lambs.

His eyes showed no fear. He was old and worn by many seasons in the mountains, well experienced with danger.

What his eyes expressed was a fierce determination to hold the territory of his choice, no matter who or what the enemy might be—hold it to the death against all invaders.

In the hour of the young male bobcat's birth, nearly a year earlier, the old gray bobcat had ignored the arrival of the second bobcat family. The reason for this was his pre-oooccupation with a mate and a litter he had sired. The old cat stayed on with his mate until the kits he had fathered were nearly grown. This is the way of adult male bobcats—to keep moving unless there is a family to raise. Now he was back and ready to reclaim his former territory.

The young bobcat's father had been gone for weeks, never needing to be challenged. He had left without urging. The old one had trailed him until the boundary between his territory and new country was crossed.

The rock slide had driven the mother bobcat and her young daughter, the male's twin, to another place—the old bobcat had not trailed them far, only enough to know the two were truly gone. Only one was left to frighten off: the young male. This one would soon be gone. The old bobcat would see to it.

The young bobcat crawled out of the den when the storm was over. He shook himself and tensed his muscles. He bent his legs to lessen the stiffness in his joints. He dropped his head and plowed nose first through drifts of snow banked against the boulder. He did this for the pure joy of feeling the coldness of new snow in his warm nostrils. His playful bounding scared up a few startled mice, which he quickly stuffed into his mouth with his front paws.

The change in the landscape brought about by the fall of snow excited the young cat. He was filled with fresh energy. The memory of his family was fading. His need for them was slipping away.

He raced crazily around the boulder, chasing something he imagined was running in front of him—a squirrel or a woodchuck or maybe a fat vole. He was on his second round of running in circles when he suddenly faced the white-whiskered old bobcat.

The young bobcat's inborn respect for age and experience stopped him in his tracks, along with a mixture of surprise and fear. He stared hard into the steady gaze of the old one before he dropped his eyes to the ground. He assumed a position of lesser importance, lowering his shoulders and whining weakly. His behavior was driven by the instinct to act submissive in the face of a bigger, older, stronger animal.

The old one remained where he was, solid and sure, unwavering in his yellow-eyed stare. It was hypnotic, this look he gave. It was stony and had the tolerance of age and long experience.

Foolish and carefree, stupid because of his youth, the young one suddenly tossed himself into the air. He leaped for one instant in a kind of whirling dance, all four feet leaving the ground. When he landed again he made a quick swish with his left leg and batted the old one on the shoulder with a snow-covered paw.

The old one remained where he was, without moving. This encouraged the young male. This was not his father, but memories of mock battles and playful spats he shared with that other male bobcat flooded into his mind. He used techniques known to him from watching, and copying, his father's moves.

The strategy seemed to work for five minutes or more. The old bobcat dodged the playful blows thrown his way, bobbing his head and now and then raising one paw or the other.

The encounter was over in a quick slash, one so sudden the young cat did not know what hit him. His chest stung and throbbed with pain and a red stain was spreading on the snow next to where he was lying on his side.

The mauling, for this was what it was, told the young male what he needed to know about what to expect next. He rolled and twisted himself upright, coating his wound with a cold patch of snow. He came to his feet and limped away, half-running, making himself scarce as quickly as he could. He turned only once to look back, to see the old one standing calm and assured, having gotten his way once more.

Six months later the young male lay flat on his side, his chest wounds long since healed. He dipped his front paws into a stream of spring water bubbling from a crack in gray stone high on a mountain two peaks from his former home. He had his own territory where he fought as necessary to keep intruders out.

He was accustomed to solitude. The urge to search for his mother and sister was gone. As an adult his habits were those of a wild creature, self-reliant in every respect.

One day he would search for a mate and kittens would be born. For a while he would hunt for his family, and provide protection. He would teach the young ones bobcat ways. Then, like his father before him, he would slip away into the high mountain passes and return to his solo life.

The One-Eyed Raven

March

A curtain of falling snow shifted and danced against the cliffs, a cloth held loose in a giant's hand. The fall of snow obscured the raven nest from the hawk who watched. The nest was a messy collection of sticks built on a rock ledge on a cliff and sheltered by an overhang of red sandstone. Three week-old raven chicks were curled in the bottom of the nest. The raven mother covered the three, protecting them from the cold and wet.

One side of the nest was exposed to the weather. The mother raven held her back to this side, creating a black-feathered wall against the elements.

A male red-tailed hawk had a nest of his own and a mate in a tree near the river below the cliffs. He had spied on the raven nest long enough to memorize the habits of the parent birds, the position of the nest on the ledge, and the best direction to approach in an attack. Even through the dense, wet veil of spring snow dropping from the sky, he would find the nest easily.

He had waited and spied and waited for the right moment to attack. This moment came during the snowstorm. On broad, tapered wings, with his head down, his eyes protected by a membrane that blocks moisture, the hawk traveled through the air to strike feet first. In the instant of the strike the hawk landed with the combined force of his body weight and his swift drop through the air.

The hawk hit the raven nest and the tendons in his shoulders stretched taut under layers of feathers. His leg muscles flexed with the fullness of his power. He was prepared to carry a baby raven away.

In seconds the hawk was in the air again, lifting up from the raven nest, his talons empty. His attack was a failure.

With the hawk coming in fast, the mother raven turned and flung herself on her back, spreading her sharp-clawed toes toward the sky. It was her only defense and it worked. She was able to deflect the hawk's talons, receiving a puncture wound herself, but not a fatal one.

Had there been no storm, no fluttering mist of flakes swirling in the air, the hawk's bold attack would have been noticed by the raven flock, a family group of forty birds sheltering from the weather in the cliffs. Many members of the flock, all but those protecting their young, would have flown out to mob him and drive him away.

Another injury, besides the mother's puncture, resulted from the hawk's attack. The point of a talon had found the eye socket of one of the young. The eye was not yet open, so newly hatched was the tiny, featherless baby.

Soon after the hawk's attack the father raven settled over the young. The mother flew to the river and dipped her wounded belly into chill riverbank mud. She sealed the hole to keep infection out.

The three raven babies, two females and one male, grew and gained strength. They squabbled over food brought to the nest by their parents. The parents showed no favorites. They dropped regurgitated prey, bits of carrion, or morsels from the garbage dump into each gaping mouth.

The eyes of the two females were soon open and shining, but only one of the young male's lids went up. This seemed not to bother him, for he behaved as the others did, with the same enthusiasm and eagerness for life.

Spring surged into full bloom. Insects hatched, and a fuzz of new green grass covered the mountain slopes and mesa tops. Snow-melt turned the river to a deep, churning stream.

The raven parents, mates for life, took turns at the nest. The female gave more hours than the male, but one or the other of them watched the young throughout each day and every night. This was their third clutch of eggs in as many years.

At six weeks the raven babies were kitten-sized and gawky. They filled the nest to capacity. Their thrashing about threatened to break the nest apart. The nestlings were now covered with strips of black pinfeathers growing

in rows. Patches of naked pink flesh showed between the rows. The bottom of the nest was soft with layers of shed down. The parents removed most of the droppings so the nest bowl was not fouled.

The young birds slept, ate, and slept again. Their gurgles, croaks, whistles, and shrieks echoed up and down the cliffs when they were awake. The air was never still in that place, where the ravens of the cliffs built their nests.

May

May is the month when wild cherries swell up green and fat. It is the month raven parents leave their chicks alone more hours each day, returning frequently with food.

The three young ravens left the nest for the first time one bright day when their parents were gone. They stood upright on the ledge, knock-kneed and unsteady. They bobbed their heads and twisted their necks around. They hunched their bony shoulders and lifted themselves up, the better to view the unfamiliar world spread before them, one far bigger than the one they had known inside the nest.

The one-eyed male had a peculiar way of tilting his head to compensate for his blind side. His gestures, lowering his head and rolling it side to side, were common to all ravens. The difference for him was that his movements were exaggerated. They were more pronounced than in his sisters and the other young ravens.

The one-eyed raven's parents, like other ravens nesting on the cliffs, often left to forage, or ride a thermal up into the sky, or settle in the cottonwoods to groom their shiny feathers.

The pair joined ravens nesting in the cottonwoods, family groups in the trees by the river, and another flock, ravens that nested in the pines at the base of the mountains. When the flocks of ravens gathered to forage, their numbers were great in the sky. The joy they exhibited in their soaring flights was plain to any eyes watching.

L eft on their own, the three flightless young ravens gathered with birds their own age to form noisy groups along the sandstone ledges of the cliffs. They hopped, flapped, and bounced awkwardly from one ledge to another, their steps hopelessly uncoordinated. The red sandstone rocks were stained white with raven droppings. Bird lime dribbled down rock surfaces to form piles that appeared to be growing out of the rocks like strange mushrooms.

Younger birds were guarded, fed, and protected by helpers, nonbreeding members of the cliff ravens, year-old juveniles, grandfathers and grandmothers—an extended family of mature birds responsible for watching vulnerable young. Relying on helpers to protect those less capable was the raven way, as it was the way of their cousins—jays, crows, and magpies.

June

O ne warm day, when the air sizzled with the electric noise of flying insects, the young raven trio climbed out of the nest to stand on the rock ledge.

The one-eyed male went first, scratching and claw-ing, tugging with his beak to pull himself out. His sisters watched him and cheered him on with cackles, gurgles, and whistling noises. He found a smooth patch of rock ledge to stand on.

His sisters soon followed him, getting their legs tan-gled in loose sticks, dried mud, strips of wire, and other nest material. The parent birds had woven chicken wire into the nest when they constructed it, to make it stay tight and secure. The condition of the nest was now such that the wire was more a hazard than a help.

The three young ravens stood in a ragged row in the shade of the sandstone overhang, quivering with nervous excitement, their wings tucked tightly against their sides. This was far from their first trip out of the safety of the nest, but the experience was always an adventure for them.

A wind came up, a funnel-shaped whirl of energy car-rying sand and dust in its teeth. The ravens on the ledge leaned close to each other. The wind was a miniature tor-nado, a dust devil. It moved sideways along the cliffs and then, in an explosive burst, swept up to the sky.

A gust of air near the top of the cone spread out like a lone finger, capturing everything in its path. One of the young female ravens was nipped off the ledge by the finger of wind and hurled to the ground. She was picked as a sin-gle berry was taken from a clutch and discarded with a broken neck at the base of the cliffs.

The cone of dust swung away, losing strength, fading

as mist does in sunlight. The two young ravens on the ledge were not aware of what the wind had taken. They blinked against the glare, shaking their heads to loosen bits of dust caught in their feathers.

Members of the flock appeared along the front of the cliffs, dipping and diving, rising and falling, eyeing the small, dark form on the ground, lifeless and still. They swung in wide circles through the air, wings flat, voices sighing. Twenty or more birds landed, sweeping gracefully out of the cloudless blue sky. They bounced on the sand as if suspended on elastic wires, leaving easy-to-see tracks with their slender toes.

In small groups of two or three the ravens came close to gaze at the one plucked from the ledge. The loss was noted in each raven brain. A silent signal passed through the group, invisible but recorded in memory. Rings of shiny dark heads bobbed and many throats uttered cackles and caws, before the ravens left that spot and flew away.

A full-grown coyote, followed by a smaller one with a bobbing gait, came and lifted the young raven off the sand in her jaws. She carried the dead raven away to a hidden alcove or crack in the rocks, there to make a meal of it.

A week after the loss of his nestmate, the one-eyed raven stood on the ledge, spread his wings, and fell away in his first voyage through the air. In this crucial moment, with just one eye and not two, his judgment over distance was clearly flawed.

He tumbled through empty space, wildly out of control for the one- hundred-and-twenty-foot drop from the

ledge to the ground. His wings were thrust back so far, flying was almost impossible. He had no sense of balance.

He crash-landed and scraped the surface of the earth
with his heels, raising a small puff of dust. Before he
breathed evenly again, the female raven, his sister, flopped
on top of him. She had taken her first plunge right after his.
She made it without hurting herself and so did the one-
eyed male.

Their free fall from the ledge began a new phase of
life for the young ravens. Babyhood was over, childhood
began. For the two ravens, childhood meant practice
flights where each bird would come near to breaking his
or her tender neck. They would suffer the indignity of
crashing into a cottonwood tree. They would bungle a
landing and hit face down in the dirt. They would whine,
wail, and complain like all raven babies when these acci-
dents happened.

When a young raven crash-lands and cries out piti-
fully, the parent birds rush to its side. They are forever on
call, to assist, feed, comfort, or simply stand by looking
sympathetic. At this early stage the young birds have the
full benefit of parental concern. In seven or eight weeks
the young fly as well as any adult, and if they have a
mishap, they will no longer expect to be rescued.

July

When not asleep in the nest, experimenting with
flight, or napping in the shade of a piñon pine, the

one-eyed raven and his sister played games and explored the world around them. They were independent, eager for each new experience, and still they pestered their parents, whimpering and begging for what scraps they could get. It was not just their own parents the two went after, calling loudly and demanding attention. They chased the parents of other ravens. Sometimes this worked, and a tidbit was tossed their way.

The edge of the river was a choice place to go, to visit with birds the same age and peck the mud for worms and mud-dwelling insects. The young ravens used their toes for scratching and probing. They played at disrupting the long, sinewy trails of determined, marching ants. With their beaks they stabbed at shiny black beetles. They pestered any creatures they discovered creeping, hopping, or crawling along.

An inch worm became a toy to tease. A stink bug was a ball to toss about. When a beetle landed helpless on its back, its legs wriggling furiously in the air, the ravens gathered to stare in curiosity and amazement. They turned their heads sharply to one side or the other, the better to observe the struggling insect.

Insects, small rodents, lizards, frogs, and toads were speared, scratched, tormented, dismembered, and sometimes swallowed. Certain insects—stinkbugs, for instance— were never tasted twice when after eating one, a stinging bitterness was sharp on a raven tongue.

Raven voices were in constant use, for this was the way these birds made contact with each other and shaped their social lives. Lively young ravens playing together by the river chorused raucously, with croaks, grumbles, screeches, and screams that echoed through the trees on summer days.

Conversations began with low grumbles that joined like strands of wool on a loom, weaving a fabric of shrill cries so pitched, no individual could be attentive to what another bird was "saying." The noisy communications of ravens teach, warn of danger, scold or praise, accept or reject. The one-eyed male was as loud as any raven gathered on the cliffs or by the river. His body was now covered in raven plumage. No naked skin showed through. His shiny black feathers were finely formed. He often pranced and displayed his neck ruff, spreading his wings away from his sides. He postured as if he were Raven Number One, the boss-bird of any less-aggressive ravens.

On warm July mornings the one-eyed raven and his sister were filled with energy. They feared nothing and were wild with hungry impatience. Morning spirits ran high, and this was the best time for flying practice. Flying (and crashing) wore out the young birds and left them sore with bumps, bruises, and tangled feathers.

In the afternoons they remained on the ground. They filled the hours chasing lizards, snakes, and mice, their tails spread and their heads held low. They looked like roadrunners pretending to be ravens.

After sunset the two birds curled in their nest, sleeping soundly with bellies rounded from an evening meal of leftovers from a coyote kill. The pair might have visited the dump and experimented with the taste of rotting human food, or dinner might have consisted of a heap of dead grasshoppers mixed with juniper berries.

August

On a day in August, one of intense heat, the one-eyed raven stood on the ground with his legs spread apart, gripping the sandy soil with his feet and scrunching warm grains between his scaly toes. His toenails were yellow. He cocked his head to see his prey better, a dung beetle going head-to-head with a dull-colored scrap of rabbit dropping. His one good eye was bright with curiosity, moist at the edges and fringed with a fine fur of dark lashes.

He got closer, lowering his sleek, shiny head, and when he did, the feather ruff at his neck splayed out. Sunlight on his feathers revealed unexpected colors— blues, ambers, and shimmery greens. Several molts would come and go before he was finished growing, before he would resemble the two-foot-long three-pound bird his father was.

The one-eyed raven viewed the beetle as a plaything, and yet like other toys in his life, it might become a bite to eat. He stabbed the beetle with the tip of his beak and tossed it into the air. It landed on its back and struggled to sort out its six legs and turn right-side up. The raven flipped the beetle a second time, sending it a foot beyond where he stood.

His sister dropped from the sky and joined him on the sand, her wings arched, her call a protest. He was having fun entertaining himself and she was left out, ignored.

He answered her with sounds from his throat that mimicked her own. First she spoke, then he did, and then she spoke again. Their voices collided and mixed. Before long the air was filled with a jangle of croaks and caws that rose up into the heat of the day. They were having a raven argument.

Their language was private, one both ravens understood in a particular way. No other ravens use quite the vocabulary nestmates share: the number of sounds in a row, the pauses and clicks, phrases that mark meaning. The two forgot about the beetle and sprang away from the ground as if set loose by springs. Soon they were shooting through the sky, rolling and diving, soaring so high they became black dots againt the blue.

October

A bobcat slinked across the floor of the cottonwood forest, passing shadowy and half-seen through a first gentle fall of snow. The leaves of the cottonwoods were yellow drops of pure gold.

The one-eyed raven and his sister perched side by side on a high branch and observeed the the bobcat's journey. It moved the way smoke travels, silent and ghostly, twisting around the trunks of the trees. The light snow formed a shimmery coating on the bobcat's fur, like a patch of lace dropped from above. An unusual quiet had settled over the cottonwood forest. Every creature near where the bobcat walked held its breath.

The one-eyed raven droped from his perch and flew low, skimming a foot or so above the ground. He zipped over the top of the bobcat's tufted ears, playfully, teasingly, without fear. The cat lifted its front legs, stretched them up and out, claws ready to grab at the nuisance that bothered him. The cat tried to bring down the pest from the sky shaped like a bullet, a creature dark and shiny that slid through the snowy air without effort.

There was no sense to it, and yet it happened that the one-eyed raven drove the cat along the ground, herding it as a mother hen will rush her chicks to safety. The one-eyed raven's sister leaned her head to one side and eyed the action below. Many members of the cottonwood flock appeared, summoned by a signal only ravens know, one that told the birds to gather and join in running the bobcat out of their territory.

The one-eyed raven was bolder after driving the bobcat away. A new strength rose in his breast. His nestmate and other companions saw a sharper glint in his one good eye.

January

On a bitter cold afternoon the one-eyed raven showed his sister how to crack river ice to get at the water underneath, stabbing at the white firmness with sharp whacks of his beak. She imitated him.

Together they broke up a small section of ice and dipped their heads into the frigid stream. They drank and then flew to a leafless cottonwood branch to perch and groom their thick, glossy feathers. The cold penetrated their chests and they shivered. Shivering warmed them and soon they were off the branch and whirling up into a white sky.

They foraged in a canyon the one-eyed male had discovered. Deer traveled up and down the canyon bottom, a ravine so narrow only two or three pines had room to grow from the top of the drainage to the lower end. The deer hovered close together for comfort and warmth in this sheltered place, struggling to find graze. They kicked at the ice and snow covering the ground, exposing last season's rank grass.

The deer felt safe in the canyon. For many winters deer had come to the same hidden-away spot. Beyond starvation, which was an ever-present danger, fear came only when mountain lions, bobcats, or black bears choose to move through the area searching for fresh meat. The big predators never passed through the canyon at the same time, but when one did, several deer might be lost out of the herd.

The first winter of the one-eyed raven's life passed with harsh freezes. Temperatures well below zero persisted all the days of January. When the sun shone, its light was nothing but a pale hint of warmth that never materialized. Winter brought death to many members of the raven clans, those too old or weak to endure days of hunger and privation.

The canyon of the one-eyed raven's discovering, with its reliable population of deer, was a gift to the ravens, bears, bobcats, and all creatures who feast on what other predators leave behind. It was the pattern of almost weekly kills made by lions, bobcats, or bears that the one-eyed raven, his sister, and any ravens who followed, depended on for their survival in the darkest weeks of winter.

When the one-eyed raven and his sister found a kill, most of it was gone to the belly of the animal that brought it down, yet there was always something left to be gnawed at. The ravens were scavengers and skilled at their task.

The one-eyed raven showed his sister how to get at the maggots and other flesh-devouring vermin that swarm when a kill appears to be completely used.

There was sweet, fatty marrow to be pecked out of the bones, parasites on the hide, and grease to scrape off strips of tissue half-rotted and ignored by predators with full bellies.

Magpies flock, fighting mad if they don't get more than their share. Eagles drop heavily out of the skies, slow to be driven off, even when coyotes come to snarl, bare their fangs, and insist they own the scraps remaining. Eagles will flap up and leave a carcass, moving heavily into the lower branches of the pines to wait while a coyote fills its empty belly. The eagles return when the coyotes are finished, to rip and tear at what little is left.The ravens acted as if they owned the kills, but of necessity they allowed others to come and go.

March

Spring brought in weather that changed from one hour to the next, like the mood of the one-eyed raven. The

skies passed from thundering and blinking with
lightning to billowing with white clouds that
sailed like mystery ships from west to
east. A freeze came. The wind blew and
the air stung with sleet. The world
was drenched in a gray wetness, a
rain that soaked down deep.

The bond between the one-eyed
raven and his sister had been so close
they appeared stitched together as if by
invisible threads. At one year of age everything changed. They quarreled, fought, and
were furious with each other. They estab-
lished separate perching trees. They dived
head over tail feathers, tormenting each
other in the air, screaming with anger and
frustration. They no longer rolled and soared
in playful flight.

The one-eyed raven hung in solitary suspension
against the cliffs, his good eye a dark glint staring. He
watched older pairs build their nests. Clutches of eggs
appeared—three, four, or sometimes six. The one-eyed
raven had no patience with his sister. She was a pest,
annoying him by trailing behind wherever he went.

Clans of ravens were everywhere making familiar
croaks and calls, acting out the rituals of mating and rear-
ing young. The one-eyed raven watched them and as he did
he experienced a break in his connection to the others.

Like so much about this sleek dark bird, with his

sightless eye and the eye that missed nothing, the severing of connections to all he had ever known was a mysterious thing. He looked to the north constantly. It had become his habit to scan that horizon with his one good eye. Something was stirring in him—an urge to go, to explore country he had never seen. He was not like the others. Birds his age do not leave, or if they do it will be in two years, or three, or five.

The raven clans weave together and pull apart, and then merge again. While this went on the one-eyed raven's home was in the north, a great distance from all that was familiar to him.

A young raven from the foothill flock mated with the one-eyed raven's sister. A nest was constructed in a pine grove above the flats where the river flows. The young from that nest grew and moved west, to join with the cliff ravens, and so it went, in raven time, on and on forever.

The Bear Orchard

The Bears

He was born in December, a single cub, an only child, naked and small, no bigger than an orange. His mother was an old-timer in the mountains. Her den was a cave carved by ancient glaciers deep in the face of a granite cliff five hundred feet above the treeline.

She slept through the birth but woke soon after, to lick her naked baby with her long pink tongue and tuck him against her chest where her nipples were. His tiny mouth wrapped around a teat, and milk soon flowed into his stomach. For weeks his eyes remained closed. He did nothing but sleep, suckle, and grow. He was unaware of any sensations beyond the satisfaction of a full belly and the security of his mother's warm body surrounding him.

His mother woke up only rarely. When she did she

roused enough to step out of the cave to relieve herself. She left him curled on a bed of moss, so little he was hard to see in the gloom of the cave interior. When she came back she took him up close again.

Octaviano

In a valley far below the bear's den, an old man with white whiskers and a sagging, wrinkled face watered and pruned the orchard. His name was Octaviano. He looked to be more than ninety years old. Nobody knew his age for sure. He barely spoke to people. He kept to himself from one end of the year to another.

Everybody said he was sour in his heart, bitter and angry over something that had happened years before. No one knew what that thing was. It had happened so long ago that the memory of it was gone like summer rain in sand. Folks old enough to remember the distant past mentioned heartbreak, maybe the death of a child or a wife. People whispered and told each other the old man was more wild than tame, a ghost or a spirit, someone happier with the company of animals in the forest than human beings.

Octaviano did not use words so much as speak with his eyes, his expression. It was plain he cared nothing for the opinions of the people of the town. The orchard was his home, his property. It had been left to him by his father, and before that to his father by his grandfather, and so on back in time.

The orchard was not only the most lush, well tended,

and beautiful of any in the mountain valley, it also produced the most fruit. The apples, pears, and peaches from
Octaviano's trees were one hundred times more delicious
and firm, more juicy and perfect, than those from any other
fruit grower's trees.

The orchard was well above the village, on a foothill
slope. If you let your eyes wander high, above and beyond
the tops of the trees, you would see the splendor of the
peaks, snow-covered even in summer.

Octaviano lived alone, the way he wanted. He slept
in a shack on the edge of the orchard, with a cot, some
pots and pans, a blanket, and a wood stove. Behind the
orchard, hidden in an aspen grove, he had built an out-
house. He cooked on the wood stove and kept warm by it
in winter. He raised vegetables in a patch of garden and
did not seem to need much besides what he could grow.
He'd come to town for groceries now and then. People
understood his wanting to be alone. People never bothered him.

The old man had a different attitude about the village
children. He liked it that they came to the orchard to visit
and play under the trees. He welcomed them and allowed
them to follow along as he worked. He gave them small
tasks, and he told them stories.

Octaviano let the children come and go as they
pleased, except in the autumn months, during harvesttime.
Beginning in September he made rules for them to obey,
sending them home before sunset, shooing them down the
trail to the village without explaining why.

The Bears

The bear cub grew quickly, as babies will, and by early spring, which comes in May to the mountains, he was up and staggering around. He moved like he might be a little drunk, but this was because of how young he was and inexperienced. He stayed close to the old sow, so near that when the two walked together it was hard to see him. He blended with her. He tucked himself against her dark, furry side and was so much a part of her no creatures of the forest knew his scent as different from her's.

To the sow this was not true. To her sensitive nose the cub had his own potent smell. When she left him alone for any length of time, in the den or outside it, she knew where he was every moment, by his distinct aroma.

For weeks after the cub opened his eyes and learned to tumble and wobble around in his baby-walking way, the sow watched over him lovingly. She let him do as he pleased, never minding his demands to nurse, even if she were busy fishing in the stream or pulling berries from a wild raspberry bush. She licked him constantly to rid his tiny, beady eyes of flies, to clean his furry little body, or to comfort him if he became frightened.

Octaviano

In May the orchard hummed with insect noise. Bumble-bees cruised close to the ground, hunting for nest sites. The time of honey-sweet blossoms fluttering in the breeze was passing. Leafed-out trees had fruit buds on their

branches, nut-hard and nearly invisible for how small they were. Only one enemy threatened the fruit trees in early spring, and that was a freeze.

Octaviano had a sure way to protect his trees from frost. He built miniature bonfires on the ground between the rows and stoked these all night, if need be. The smoke and heat kept frost crystals from growing.

On bright, cold mornings in May you could see ice on the ponds and in the ditches, but the trees, with their tender buds a promise of what was coming, were safe.

The children came to watch Octaviano set up his fires. They helped by stacking slender sticks of pine and cedar in piles, making shapes like pretend watchtowers. Octaviano cut shavings with his big knife for kindling. The children chattered constantly while they worked, asking the old man a million questions. Octaviano might not be willing to string three words together for the sake of a grown person, but the children got him talking.

He told the children about animals that lived in the mountains around the village. Some, like wild sheep, they had never seen with their own eyes. He had special knowledge of wild creatures, knowing the secret ways of foxes, bobcats, coyotes, and great horned owls. Mostly he knew about bears.

When he talked about bears a thing beyond the ordinary happened. The children found themselves cast under a spell by his bear stories. The words he spoke about these animals became bright images dancing in front of their eyes, as if they were seeing bears in the flesh. The children wondered why his bear stories were so hypnotic. They discussed these things going home from the orchard.

They said words to each other like, "Maybe the old man was a bear in disguise and that's how he comes to know so much about them."

"Maybe he was raised by bears, like the twins who were brought up by wolves."

"He might be a medicine man who belongs to the Bear Clan," one child suggested.

The children went home pondering the mysterious power of the old man's bear stories. If they went home puzzled, they also went home happy.

The Bears

By late August the cub was big enough to scramble up trees and make the trunks sag earthward with his weight. He liked drawing his claws down the sides of aspen trees to make deep grooves in the sweet-smelling bark.

He dug in the ground next to anthills and used a stick, the same way his mother did, to poke into the ant nest. Ants scurried up the stick unaware they were on their way to being eaten.

The cub learned new skills from his mother each day. Her scoldings taught him as much as her patient demonstrations of how to catch a fish, or how to peel layers off a honeycomb to get at the slippery, sticky sweetness inside, or the best way to pick rosehips without getting pricked by thorns.

He followed her or waited for her to come back when she went off on a personal mission without him. When she left him alone he curled up in a mass of brown fur, safe in a hidden spot. He stayed in that place until she was back, secure in the certainty of her return. He trusted her. The old sow was the center of his bear universe.

In the last days of August the two bears traveled north, miles from the den where the cub had been born. The old sow started one morning, loping with a smooth, flowing stride. The cub ran to keep up.

This late in summer many thunderstorms had come and gone, bringing heavy rain and the blue-green flash of lightning. Wildflowers bloomed across every meadow, and grew thick along even the narrowest stream bed. The flower heads tossed brightly in the wind. Marmots scampered from one clump of grass to another, foraging for bedding to keep their winter hibernation dens warm and cozy.

The sow caught gophers and ground squirrels with quick swipes of her huge paws. She shared these morsels with the cub. He caught mice on his own, and one water snake out of a silvery stream that spilled from a crack between two gray boulders.

They saw a bobcat, only a

brief glimpse, and made short work of a sheep carcass they discovered in a ravine. The sheep had strayed from a near-by flock and a coyote had killed it.

Two days into this trip, the mother bear ordered the cub, in a particular way she had of growling and snarling, to stay put and not follow her. She signaled he was to wait and assured him, with grunts and murmurs, that she would soon be back.

Octaviano

Early in September Octaviano stood in the middle of his orchard and admired the fruit ripening on his trees—pears, apples, and peaches. This would be one of his best years.

The children came with their questions. They asked why he let swarms of wasps, bees, and flies bore into the peaches and make holes with brown edges. They wanted to know why he let the branches droop to the ground, so animals prowling in the orchard—coyotes and raccoons—could take as much of the fruit as they wanted. And why didn't he scare the birds away, like other growers did? Magpies and jays perched boldly on the fruit and tore out fat chunks with their beaks.

Octaviano explained how he felt, that the orchard produced enough fruit for every living thing, more than enough if you thought about it. There was fruit left over for taking to town in wooden crates, for selling by the roadside, for canning. That was the truth of it. They nodded, and yet secretly wondered about the old man who so willingly shared what he treasured most in the world.

The Bears

When the old sow returned to the spot where she had left the cub she acted differently than she had before. She was growly and in a bad temper. She did not smell the same. A new and unfamiliar aroma hung about her. Although she was gray around the muzzle, the sow had mated while she was gone.

The two bears turned for home, the cub wary because of the change he sensed in his mother.

He quickly forgot about the change when a storm swept in over the mountains, dropping snow that layered two feet in the high places where no trees grew. The bears took temporary shelter in a shallow cave cut into a rock face. They spent a night in the cave before getting home. After one day in the den, resting, nibbling berries, and wriggling on grass damp with snow-melt, the bears were on the move again. This time they headed down the mountain toward the valley and the village far below.

The cub had grown huge. He weighed two hundred pounds. Much of this was fur and fat, but he was well muscled and strong. He lumbered after his mother, as he had done when no more than a tiny cub. The old sow kept a steady pace on the trail, following it as if she'd done the same a hundred times. For the cub it was all new and surprising. The smells and sights of the lowlands distracted and enticed the young bear. The closer they came to the valley, the sweeter were the aromas drifting into his nose.

Octaviano

Octaviano lay on his cot in the evening hour of a September day. He was bone-weary. His old joints ached. He rubbed his chin and listened for the sounds he knew would come, the rustling and huffing noises of bears moving into the orchard, their heavy, irregular breathing. They came, as they always did in the autumn months, for their share of the fruit.

The old man had sent the children home early, to make sure none saw a bear. He knew what would happen if he were not careful about this. The children would rush to tell their parents. The parents would come up the trail with guns to shoot the bears, saying these wild, dangerous animals were too close to the village for safety.

Funny, he thought, the older he got the more he felt like a bear and not a person any longer. He shared what he could with the bears, the bounty of fruit he could not make use of himself. In his mind it was the right thing to do.

The Bears

The young bear stood next to his mother at the edge of the orchard, intoxicated by the smells coming up off the valley, the rank smell of water in the ponds and ditches, the heady perfume of fresh-cut hay. His head was spinning. The old sow, seeing the signs, whacked him on the shoulder with her paw. She was still in charge.

The two bears stood on their hind legs, shoulders touching, swinging their heads and looking for any movement that warned of danger. They saw three adult bears, strangers to them, shadowy in the dusk. The bears were coming into the orchard from the south.

The gathering night was still but for the breathing of the bears and the noise of their heavy tread through dry grass and fallen leaves. The old sow had been coming to the orchard every year of her life. Before that her mother had come, and before that her mother's mother. It was a thing the bears did every fall of every year, as much a constant for them as mating, or finding a den to spend the winter in.

The young bear could not contain his eagerness. His mouth was watering. Drool clung to his furry chin. He lunged on all fours down the steep slope into the orchard, and this time his mother let him go.

The Orchard

The old man lay on his cot and closed his eyes, remembering the day he shot the bear. He counted in his mind. Could it be eighty years past? It seemed impossibly long ago. But it was true. He had turned thirteen when he killed the bear. He was ninety-three now.

Eighty years. An eternity. He was sure he had not made up for the killing, though he had tried for every one of those eighty years. His father had been a great hunter and had taught his only son to kill with a gun. In those long-gone days Octaviano's father was his hero.

It was traditional for a boy to honor his father and try to be like him, to mimic everything the elder man did. Octaviano was no exception to this. He practiced hard to become skilled with a gun, even when the voice in the back of his mind told him he could never be like his father, no matter how hard he tried. Deep down he was different. He hated killing animals. He knew killing wild game was the way mountain people fed themselves winter meat. Still, he hated it.

Octaviano's old bones shook when he remembered the day his father proudly gave him the first rifle he could call his own, saying, "Now you are ready to kill a bear." They went together into the mountains, to a place Octaviano's father knew by heart where bears gathered to take fish out of the river. Sure enough the bears arrived, and when the moment came for the boy to pull the trigger he could not. He froze. His father gripped him by the shoulder and whispered, "Do it. Shoot!"

The Bears

All the bears in the orchard, including the old sow and her cub, paid no heed to each other. They were too busy eating, stuffing their mouths with sweet, moist fruit.

They sat on the ground and scooped up windfalls. They pulled fruit from over their heads, or they climbed up the trunks to straddle a split between branches and pluck fruit dangling from the spread limbs. It was midnight before the bears slowly moved off into the forest, their bellies swollen and full from feasting.

Octaviano

The old man lay on his cot, still as death, and remembered. He saw in his mind's eye the terrible damage he had done to the bear, the bear he shot because his father told him he must. He had delayed, hesitated, and in this way he gave warning to the bears. They turned to run and only then did he let loose his shot, striking a bear in the shoulder, ripping out a section of muscle and bone. The bear, badly injured, kept running.

They trailed the wounded animal for three days, following and hoping it would die. Instead it found the strength to run, and in the high passes, coming along behind, they heard it scream in pain. Finally they came to where the wounded bear was hiding, under a rock ledge, whimpering and weak from losing so much blood. Octaviano's father put the bear out of its misery, plainly ashamed of his son's failure to make a clean kill.

Octaviano had never again lifted the gun. He brought further shame to his family with his refusal to hunt. His father hardly spoke to him, so angry was he to have a son who would not help kill elk and deer, the winter meat supply for the village. His father died without understanding how Octaviano felt about killing. In Octaviano's remembering, pairs of eyes drifted before him, bear eyes, small, brown, round, and filled with a soft, sad light. He had tried all these years to make up for his mistake, and to banish the vision of the bear eyes.

The Bears

The old sow and her cub lumbered up the mountain, returning to the den. Both bears were dull-witted, their senses numbed from the fullness in their bellies.

For one more long winter season the two bears shared the den where the cub had been born. In the coldest, dreariest time of all, a new cub made its way into the world.

When the year turned and spring came it was time for the young male to move off and live on his own. He was slow to go, jealous of the newcomer. He hung around the den and pestered his mother, demanding attention. She growled at him, snapping and slashing with her claws, impatient to be rid of him.

Finally he went away for good, to search out his own territory, to find a mate, to become the sire of cubs. His chances of living to a great old age were strong because his mother had taught him everything useful that she knew.

Index